Barry Loser

and the with PETS

poo bag

Thing on cover always happens to

Jim Smith

Sausage dog

As far back as I can remember, I've always wanted a sausage dog. They're like two of my favourite things squidged together - a sausage and a dog!

woof

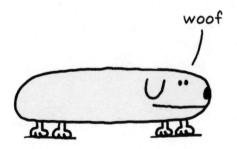

Here are some other pets I've always wanted:

pizza cat

cheeseburger
hamster

spaghetti
Bolognese
stick insect

I don't think any of those exist though.

If I did get a sausage dog I'd teach it some amazekeel tricks:

fetching the remote control

acting like a foot stool

being a hairy skateboard →

But first I've got to badger my mum about it non-stop until she buys me one. Which is what this story is about.

Chapter one, I mean two

It all started a couple of weeks ago when I saw a poster stuck to a lamp post on Mogden High Street. The poster said:

SAUSAGE DOG FOR SALE!
Call Gladys Foo
on 555 1485
for more info.

'Look, Mum!' I said, pointing at the poster. We were walking home from school, which is something I usually do with my best friends Bunky and Nancy, except this time my mum had dragged me into Mogden Town to do some boring old shopping instead.

who's this Loser?

She stopped pushing the buggy, which had my little brother, Desmond Loser the Second, strapped inside it, and peered at the poster.

'Gladys Foo?' chuckled my mum, carrying on walking. 'That's a funny old name isn't it.'

I thought about reminding my mum that her surname was 'Loser', and how before she'd married my dad it'd been 'Harumpadunk'. But I had more important things to be getting on with than that.

Miss Harumpadunk

Mrs Loser

I opened my mouth and got ready to do some serious badgering.

Operation Badger

Have you noticed how, when you're thinking about something a lot, like sausages and dogs for example, they keep popping up everywhere you look?

That's what started happening next.

We'd only walked as far as the next
lamp post, when what did I see but a
totally normal, boring old dog weeing
up against it.

not
embarrassed
at all

'Check it out!' I said, starting to
badger my mum. 'A little doggy
having a wee wee. Do you know
what that reminds me of?'

12

My mum peered down at me. 'Do you need the toilet, Barry?' she asked.

actually do need wee

'No mum, I don't need the toilet,' I sighed, and we carried on walking until we got to Bruce the butcher's and I spotted a string of plastic sausages hanging up in the window.

'Oh my unkeelness,' I said, pointing at the fake bangers. 'Plastic sausages! Can you guess what they make me think of, Mum?'

My mum gave me a funny look, like
she thought I was trying to tell her
I needed a poo or something. 'Half a
dozen sausages please Bruce,' she said
to the butcher.

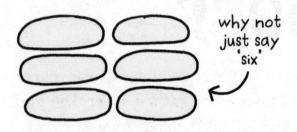

why not
just say
'six'

'MU-UM!' I said, trying to get her
attention.

'WHAT, Barry?' snapped my mum.

'Well,' I said. 'You know how you're
buying sausages right now?'

'Just get to the point,' sighed my
mum.

'I WANT A SAUSAGE DOG!' I cried.

Bruce the butcher handed my mum her sausages. 'That's a fiver for you, Losers,' he said, doing a wink.

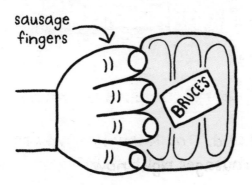

sausage fingers

BRUCE'S

'No chance!' said my mum, but I don't think she was talking to Bruce.

We walked out of the butcher and started heading home. 'Looking forward to the disco, Barry?' asked my mum, because it was the Mogden School Valentine's Day Disco tonight.

'Yeah I spose,' I said, wondering if I should give up badgering her for a sausage dog and try for a spaghetti Bolognese stick insect instead.

School disco

'Barry!' cried Bunky as I walked into Mogden School Hall nine trillion hours later.

Coloured lights were flashing round the edge of the room and music was blaring out of two ginormous speakers. Balloons bounced around on the dance floor and a black box hanging off the ceiling pumped purple clouds of smoke into the air.

In the corner of the hall, standing behind a table, was Mrs Dongle the school secretary.

'This is DJ Dongles coming at ya on the ones and twos!' she warbled into a microphone.

Then she pressed a button on her music player and the **Future Ratboy** theme tune started playing through the speakers.

Future Ratboy, in case you didn't know, is my all-time favourite TV show. It's all about this kid who gets zapped to the future and transformed into a half boy, half rat, half TV.

'Future Ratkeels!' I cried, sticking my hand out in front of me like I was holding a dog lead, and I jiggled towards Bunky, my bum wagging like it had a tail.

'What in the name of unkeelness are you doing, Barry?' laughed Nancy Verkenwerken, who was standing next to Bunky.

'It's the Doggy Walk Wiggle!' I said, skidding to a stop next to them both.

Nancy chuckled. 'How's the badgering going?' she asked. I'd told her all about me badgering my mum for a sausage dog, of keelse.

'Hasn't worked yet unfortukeely,'
I said, my nose drooping.

Bunky patted me on the shoulder and
grabbed a Cherry Fronkle from a
pyramid of cans that'd been stacked
up on a table.

'Have a Fronkle instead,' he said, like
he'd bought it for me.

Just then, Anton Mildew marched
past, doing his world famous robot
dance. 'MUST. DESTROY. ALL.
BALLOONS,' he bleeped, and Nancy
chuckled.

I cracked my can of Fronkle open
and took a sip. 'Fancy a boogie,
Bazza?' said a familikeels voice.

I twizzled round and spotted
Sharonella Sharalumbus from my
class, standing three millimetres away
from the end of my nose. Next to
her was her friend Fay Snoggles.

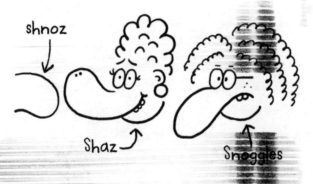

shnoz

Shaz

Snoggles

'NO WAY!' I spluttered, Fronkle
spraying all over her and Fay's shoes.

Sharonella fluttered her eyelashes
at me. 'Lemme know if you change
your mind,' she said, dancing off,
and I shuddered like a dog who's just
finished a wee.

Smoochy dance time

After that I jiggled around on the dance floor, doing the Doggy Walk Wiggle with Bunky and Nancy for about nineteen hours. Then all of a non-sudden the song we were dancing to stopped.

Mrs Dongle tapped the microphone with one of her shiny red nails. 'And now something for all you lovers out there!' boomed her voice through the speakers.

'Yuck, did you hear that?' I said, pretending to puke all over Bunky and Nancy's trainers. 'DJ Dongles just called us lovers!'

Mrs Dongle pressed a button and a Frankie Teacup song started to warble out of the speakers.

Banana Moon

Frankie Teacup is my dad's favourite singer, in case you didn't know. He's so old he isn't even alive anymore.

Dad's fave tea towel

Frankie Teacup

& the Saucers

'Ooh, Banana Moon - that's my gran's favourite!' squawked Sharonella, and she twizzled round on the spot, looking for someone to have a smoochy jiggle with.

I stepped backwards a millimetre, remembering how she'd fluttered her eyelashes at me earlier. 'Let's get the keelness out of here,' I cried, grabbing Bunky and Nancy and zooming off the dance floor.

The snack table

'Hide!' I whispered, zig-zagging over to the huge triangle of Cherry Fronkle cans, which by the way was right next to the emergency exit.

'Hey!' shouted Bunky, skidding to a stop. 'I was enjoying that song.' He looked back at the dance floor where Anton was still doing his loserish robot dance.

'What are you, crazy?' I said, ducking behind the cans. 'You wanna end up dancing with a GIRL?'

'Or even worse - a BOY!' said Nancy, pretending to puke all over my trainers.

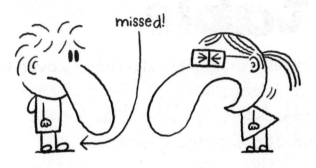

missed!

Gordon Smugly, who's the smuggest, ugliest person in our class, wandered up to us.

'It's dangerous out there,' he said, plucking a salt and vinegar crisp out of a ginormous bowl and slotting it into his annoying mouth. 'I had to get off the dance floor before Sharonella pounced on me.'

'Oh please,' said Nancy. 'Even Shazza's not that desperate.'

Stuart Shmendrix, who's sort of like Gordon's sidekick, trundled over all sweatily. 'Phew, that was close,' he said, grabbing a Cherry Fronkle. 'Did you see the way Fay Snoggles was staring at my bum?'

'Listen to you losers!' chuckled Bunky. 'What are you afraid of?' And he bopped back on to the dance floor.

'Be careful, Bunky!' I cried, but it was too late, he was gone.

Invisible lasso

Stuart cracked his Fronkle open and me, him, Nancy and Gordon watched all loserishly as Bunky waggled his legs around on the dance floor.

Sharonella and Fay were circling him like cats about to pounce on a very stupid, bum-wiggling mouse.

I rested my hand on the lever that opens the emergency exit door, getting ready to escape if Shazza spotted me. 'Poor old Bunkster,' I said. 'Silly doggy doesn't know how much trouble he's in.'

Bunky's sort of like my human pet dog, in case that last bit sounded weird.

Bunky the human dog

Just then, Darren Darrenofski from our class wobbled out of the boys' toilets. He was doing his flies up while holding a Fronkle at the same time, which isn't an easy thing to do.

'Darren!' whisper-shouted Stuart. 'Get over here before the girls spot you.'

But Frankie Teacup was singing too loud for Darren to hear.

'Hey, what's Shazza doing?' said Nancy, and I spotted her on the dance floor, swinging an invisible lasso around in the air like she was a cowgirl.

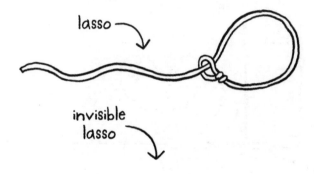

lasso

invisible lasso

'That's a funny old dance move isn't it,' I said, sounding like a bit of a granny, and I treated myself to a cheese and onion crisp for being so loserish.

'The woman's gone completely stark raving bonkers,' said Gordon, not that I was listening to him.

I was too busy spotting one of Nancy's trainers.

What Nancy's trainer was doing

'What in the name of unkeelness?'
I gasped, staring at Nancy's left foot.
'Your trainer - it's . . . tapping to
the music!'

'Careful Nance,' chuckled Gordon.
'You'll be dancing with Mildew next.'

Nancy rolled her eyes. 'As if, Smugly,' she said, and I tried to spot Bunky on the dance floor, but he'd disappeared behind a cloud of purple smoke.

Over on the other side of the room, Darren finished zipping his flies and looked up. Suddenly he froze - Sharonella was staring straight at him.

iced Daz

'You're mine, Darrenofski!' she
screeched over the top of Banana
Moon, lassoing her invisible rope
around his neck and starting to
pretend-pull him towards her.

Darren started to edge backwards.
He dropped his Fronkle can and
a pink fizzy puddle spread out
underneath his trainers.

'Man down!' cried Stuart, watching as Darren's trotter slipped in the Fronkle.

He flapped his hands like a pig trying to fly and Sharonella whipped behind him, catching him in her arms.

A nose poked out of a purple cloud and Anton appeared at our table.

'May I have the pleasure of this boogie?' he said in his normal, loserish voice, and he shot his robot hand out to Nancy.

I peered down at Nancy's tapping foot, then up to her smiling face.

'Oh why the keelness not!' she said, grabbing Anton's hand and swooshing on to the dance floor.

'Nancy!' I cried, not that there was time for that - Fay was too busy zig-zagging up to my other best friend.

'Bunky!' I shouted. 'Watch out, Snoggles is coming to get you!'

But Bunky just ignored me and started dancing with her.

Monday morning

You know how in TV shows they just cut to a few days later?

That's what happened next - suddenly it was Monday morning and I was walking into my classroom at school.

'Oh my days, how brillz was that disco, Fay?' squawked Sharonella's voice, and I looked over to where her and Fay Snoggles usually sit next to each other.

The only thing was, Fay wasn't sitting next to Sharonella at this exact millisecond in the history of the universe - she was sitting next to . . .

BUNKY!

'Erm, there seems to have been some kind of terrible mix up here,' I said, walking over to my seat, which if you haven't worked it out yet is where Fay had plonked her bum.

'Hi Barry,' grinned Fay. 'Nigel said
I could sit next to him today.'

Nigel Zuckerberg is Bunky's real-life
name, in case you didn't know.

I looked at Bunky and he smiled up at
me, the way a naughty doggy does
to its owner.

him
again!

'Hmm, yes, well,' I said all carefully,
trying not to get too annoyed. After
all, it was just a silly old chair. 'If you
don't mind, could you pop back over
to your own seat please?'

'This area's reserved for the Shazzonofskis,' snapped Sharonella, plomping her handbag down in the chair next to her. 'That's me and Darren's names squidged together,' she said, fluttering her eyelashes at me. 'Me and you coulda been the Losernellas if you'd played your cards right, Baz.'

I breathed in through my nostrils all slowly, the way my mum does when I'm badgering her about buying me a sausage dog. 'Very well,' I said. 'I'll sit next to Nancy.'

'SEAT. TAKEN.' bleeped a familikeels voice, and I spotted Anton Mildew perched next to my other best friend.

both got glasses →

'So wait a millisecond,' I said, trying to work out where I was going to sit. Then I realised it was where Anton usually sits, which is right at the front of the classroom, next to his invisible friend, Invis.

'Oh well that's just blooming brilliant,' I mumbled, plonking my bum down and getting ready for the worst week ever.

Worst week ever

The whole rest of the week was just like Monday morning, except dotted around in different bits of school.

Like lunch on Tuesday in the canteen when Bunky & Fay and Nancy & Anton and the Shazzonofskis all sat together on a six man table (even though none of them are men).

'Come dine with us, Barold,' said Gordon, who was sitting next to Stuart. So I squidged in with them, feeling like even more of a loser than my surname.

And in the boys' changing rooms on Wednesday when we were getting ready for P.E. and Bunky, Darren and Anton spent the whole time shouting over the wall to Nancy, Sharonella and Fay.

'Can you keep the noise down please,'
I grumbled, sounding like an old
granny. 'I'm trying to get changed.'

'Keep your pants on, Loser!' snarfled
Darren, blowing Sharonella a kiss
which rebounded off the wall and
fell into one of his stinking shoes.

Then on Thursday at break time
when I headed over to the corner of
the playground to peer through the
fence into the back garden of the
old lady me and Bunky spy on while
she talks to her plants.

so
bored

'What in the name of unkeelness is
SHE doing here?' I gasped, spotting
Fay Snoggles's bum next to my best
friend's. Both of them were bent in
half, looking through the fence and
sniggling.

Fay turned round and grinned her annoying grin. 'Hi Barry,' she said. 'Afraid there's only room for two.'

'Yeah I know,' I said, walking off. 'Me and Bunky.'

And don't even get me started about Friday, when we were walking home from school and I pointed out a ginormous dog poo on the pavement right in front of Bunky's foot.

The Friday poo story

'Hey Bunky, why don't you tread in that great big stinking old pile of dog poo!' I giggled.

Me and Bunky are always telling each other to tread in dog poos like that on our walks home - it's part of what makes us so hilarikeel.

Bunky zig-zagged round the poo and was just about to do a sniggle about what I'd said when Fay walk-leaned against him. 'Yuck, I hate treading in dog poos,' she said. 'They stink.'

Bunky nodded all seriously. 'Yeah, they are pretty disgusting,' he agreed, and because of the way I was staring at him in disbelief while gasping at the same time, I almost trod in the dog poo myself.

'Oh yeah, because I was really being serious about Bunky treading in it,' I said, hearing a squelching noise behind me. I twizzled round and spotted Anton's foot, squidged right in the middle of the poo I was just talking about.

whole entire shoe inside it

'Well that's blinking brilliant isn't it,' said Anton in his non-robot voice. He hobbled over to the kerb and scraped his shoe against it. 'Just my flipping luck.'

Nancy chuckled, the way she used to when I trod in dog poos back in the good old days. 'You're funny, Mr Mildew,' she smiled, which is what she'd started calling him.

'Thank you, Mrs V,' he said. 'But that's not going to stop my blooming trainer from smelling of poo, is it.'

We carried on walking and I noticed a gooseberry bush sticking its branches through a fence, trying to grab passers-by.

I picked one of its prickly green fruits. 'A gooseberry for a gooseBarry,' I mumbled to myself, because 'gooseberries' are what people call other people who haven't been paired up with someone else.

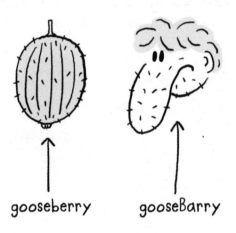

gooseberry   gooseBarry

A lamp post was standing next to me and I spotted a sign stuck to it, telling people not to let their dogs do poos on the pavement.

I thought back to the sausage dog sign I'd seen with my mum a couple of weeks before and clicked my fingers. 'Of keelse,' I whispered to myself. 'That's the answer to my gooseßarryness - pairing up with a real-life dog!'

And I plopped the gooseberry into my mouth then immedikeely spat it out again because it was really, really sour.

Sausage dog o'clock

After that I ran home at seven trillion billimetres per hour, blowing off with excitement the whole way there.

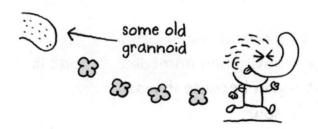

some old grannoid

'Honey, I'm ho-ome!' I cried as I strolled into the kitchen, which is what my mum's favourite TV star, Detective Manksniff, says when he walks into his house.

'Ooh-ooh, Barry,' chuckled my mum. She was bent in half, reaching into the oven with a pair of tongs. 'Did you have a nice day?'

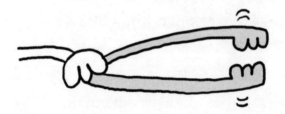

'Not really,' I said, peering into the oven. And that's when I almost weed and pooed myself right there on the spot.

'By the power of sausage dogs!'
I gasped, spotting six sizzling sausages
inside the oven.

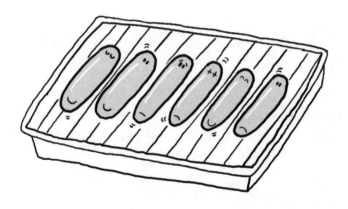

'Sausages in the oven?' I grinned,
thinking how my mum must've been
down Bruce the butcher's again -
that or she was cooking me week-old
sausages for dinner. 'It must be
a sign!'

My mum closed her eyes and breathed in very slowly through her nostrils.

Which in case you weren't listening earlier, is what she does when she knows I'm about to start badgering.

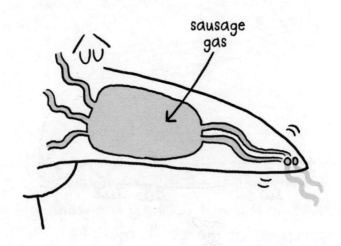

sausage
gas

'Seeing sausages in an oven is not a sign your mum's going to buy you a sausage dog, Barry,' she said.

I took a deep breath and got ready to do the biggest badger in the history of badgerisation.

like this big —

'But I really, **REALLY** want a sausage dog!' I said.

The idea of a dog

I waited a couple of milliseconds and was just about to open my mouth to ask if I could have a sausage dog again when my mum opened HER mouth, which is about twice the size of mine, so hers won.

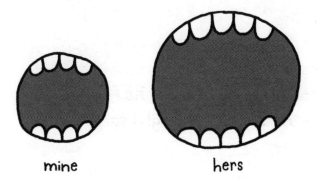

mine   hers

'You know what, Barry?' she said, pulling a can of Feeko's baked beans out of a cupboard. 'I think you just like the idea of having a sausage dog.'

'The idea?' I said, a thought bubble bubbling up above my head with a sausage dog inside it. 'Since when can you pat an idea on the head?'

66

My mum thought for a second, and I stared up at her giant hairdo, trying to see if I could spot what she was thinking inside it.

exackerly like thought bubble →

'Do you remember when you wanted that action figure of the monster thingy out of **Future Ratboy**?' asked my mum.

'Gozo?' I said, which is the name of the giant vending machine monster Mr X builds in my favourite ever **Future Ratboy** episode, '**Future Ratboy** and the Quest for the Missing Thingy'.

I rewound my brain to last year, when I'd badgered my mum to buy me the Gozo action figure for about seven weeks until she'd given in from tiredness and got me it from Roy's Toys on Mogden High Street.

My mum nodded while peeling the lid off the baked beans. 'And where's Gozo now?' she asked.

'Erm . . .' I said, glancing around. 'I think I saw his arm in the toy bucket next to the bath?'

'Exactly,' said my mum. 'You played with him for about two days, then you were on to the next thing you wanted.'

'A dog isn't a toy, Barry,' she carried on, sounding like one of the stickers my granny's boyfriend, Mr Hodgepodge, sticks in the back window of his scratched-up old car.

'You can't just play with it for a few days then forget about it.'

I stared up at mum and realised something terrible - she'd started badgering me not to badger her!

Battle of the badgerers

'Oh I get it,' I said, sounding like my mum's favourite TV star, Detective Manksniff, when he's up against one of the baddies in his TV show. 'So you wanna play it like that, do you?'

'Nothing you can say will make me buy you a sausage dog, Barry,' said my mum, pulling a tray of chips out of the grill bit of the oven.

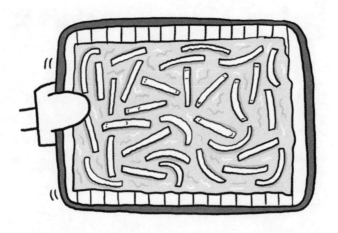

'Brillikeels,' I mumbled to myself. 'My friends have all paired off with each other and my mum won't even buy her gooseberryish son a dog to make up for it.'

My mum paused. 'Everything alright with Bunky and Nancy?' she asked. 'I haven't seen them around much this week.'

my nose

'Yeah,' I said, not wanting to talk about it. Even though I had just mumbled about it.

'You know you can tell me if something's upsetting you, don't you Snookyflumps,' said my mum, giving me a peck on the cheek.

That's the annoying thing about mums - they can always tell when something's wrong.

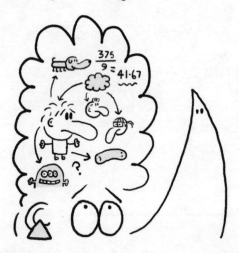

'Everything. Is. FINE!' I said, wiping her kiss off my cheek and coming up with my next amazekeel badger.

Best badger ever

'Alright then,' I said. 'Not only will I pick up all my brand new sausage dog's poos, I'll take it for a walkypoos two times a day too.'

'But you hate going for walks!' said my mum. 'All you ever do is moan the whole time.'

'I LOVE going for walks,' I lied. I hate going for walks.

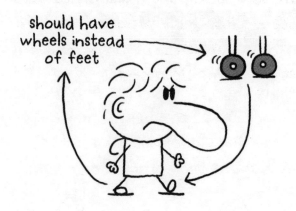

should have wheels instead of feet

My brain rewound to the bit seventeen milliseconds earlier where she'd said she wanted to get the dinner cooked.

'Also,' I said, 'I will cook my brand new sausage dog all its food. AND bath it once a week, AND tuck it up in its little basket every nightypoos!'

'What about if it starts barking in the middle of the night?' said my mum, scattering the chips on to two plates - a keel **Future Ratboy** one for me and a rubbish old kiddywinkle-ish plastic one for Desmond.

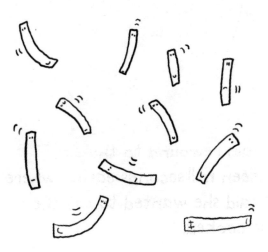

'Not a problemo,' I smiled. 'I love getting up in the middle of the night. And I simply ADORE the sound of barking!'

My mum rolled her eyes. Then she rolled two sausages on to my plate and one on to Des's. 'Desmond, dinner's ready!' she shouted, and Des trundled into the kitchen, a trail of dribble zig-zagging behind him like snail slime.

My mum picked him up and slotted him into his baby chair.

'You do know that dogs stink, don't you, Barry?' she said, starting up the badgering again.

I think she might've been beginning to quite enjoy it actukeely.

I pointed at Des. 'He stinks too,' I said.
'But I still love the little Loser.'

Des blew a raspberry in my face, and
I wondered if I did actukeely love
him, or if it was just something I said
because you're supposed to.

'And don't forget,' said my mum, sounding like even more of a badgerer than me, 'you won't be able to go everywhere with your pals if you've got a dog.'

full badger mode

She plonked the plates of sausages, chips and beans down in front of me and Des and waddled over to the sink to start washing up.

I stuffed a sausage into my face hole. 'What are you even badgering on about?' I said, bits of sausage raspberrying into Desmond's face.

still got bath time to do

'Well what if Bunky and Nancy were going to the movies or something?' said my mum, scrubbing baked bean juice off a saucepan. 'You can't take a sausage dog into a cinema, you know.'

I scooped a baked bean on to the end of a chip, making the whole thing look like a giant match.

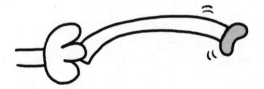

'Yeah well, I don't think they'll be inviting old Barry Loser along now they've got Anton and Fay to go with,' I said, throwing the squidgy match into my mouth and it exploded, blowing my whole entire head off.

Granny & Hodge

That last bit didn't really happen, by the way. What did happen was, there was a knock at the door.

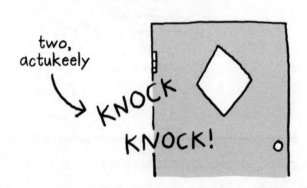

two, actukeely

KNOCK KNOCK!

'What'd you just say, Barry?' asked my mum, who was still washing up.

'Huh?' I said, stuffing sausage number two into my mouth and getting up to answer the door.

Usually my mum'd tell me not to leave the table, but this time I think she was more worried about her little Snookyflumps being okay.

'That thing about Nancy and Bunky not inviting you to the cinema,' she said as I headed down the hall.

'Nothing,' I called back, spotting two very familikeels outlines through the wobbly glass in the front door.

'Granny Harumpadunk!' I cried, opening the door and peering up her wrinkly old nostrils.

'Ooh hello my little Loser!' she warbled, giving me a stinky cuddle.

Standing next to her was her boyfriend, Mr Hodgepodge, who I don't know if I've mentioned it before but used to be my teacher eight million years ago.

'Afternoon, Loser,' he said, like we were still at school.

My mum appeared in the hallway, a tea towel hanging over her shoulder. 'Hello Mum, hello Hodge,' she said all tiredly. 'Ready for the big trip?'

My granny and Mr Hodgepodge were off on another one of their boring old cruises the next day, which was probably why they'd popped round to say hello.

everyone having a nap

'Ooh yes, we're just popping round to say goodbye,' said Granny.

getting ready to say it

Desmond Loser the Second trundled round the corner, holding a sausage. 'Hav you got me anyfing?' he gurgled, which is his way of saying hello to Granny Harumpadunk.

'Desmond, don't be so rude!' said my mum.

Granny Harumpadunk bent over
and reached her creaky arm out,
pinching Des's cheek.

really
old

really
young

She straightened back up all slowly
then blinked, her nose drooping.

'Blow me down with a pair of
knickers, I've just remembered
something,' she cooed. 'I forgot to get
the kiddywinkles a going away gift!'

My mum, who was still wearing her washing-up gloves, scratched her nose and it squeaked.

'Don't worry about that, Mum,' she said. 'You don't have to buy them something just because you're going away.'

'Oh I don't know about that,' I said, swallowing the last bit of my sausage.

Badgering grannies

If there's one thing I know, it's this: grannies are the easiest things to badger in the whole wide world amen.

All you have to do is tell them what you want, wait a couple of days and it turns up - usually wrapped inside a wrinkly old hand.

'Mum won't buy me a sausage dog,'
I said straight out, just like that. And
I peered up at Granny Harumpadunk.

She looked down at her grandson,
who was me, and somewhere inside
her fluffy grey brain, a button with
'BUY BARRY A SAUSAGE DOG' written
on it was pressed.

Now, I knew Granny Harumpadunk wasn't going to buy me a real-life sausage dog - she was only going away on a stupid little cruise, after all.

But I could probably squeeze a toy one out of her.

all covered in spit

94

'It's really annoying, because I've always wanted a sausage dog,' I carried on. 'Of keelse, I don't expect a real-life sausage dog or anything like that. But a cuddly one - that'd be nice. Or plastic if they haven't got any of those.'

not really good enough

'Stop badgering your poor old gran, Barry,' said my mum, but Granny Harumpadunk just ignored her. She was already working out where she could buy me a sausage dog toy.

'I've seen them for sale in Roy's Toys,'
I said. 'It's located at 123 Mogden High
Street, opening hours 9 till 6 every
day except Sundays, which is 11 till 4.'

This was true – I'd spotted a cuddly
sausage dog in Roy's Toys a few days
earlier when I'd been window shopping.

'You could just make it there before he shuts if you leave now,' I said. 'Not that I'm hurrying you or anything.'

My mum yoinked me back by the collar, like I was HER sausage dog.

'Alright, that's more than enough out of you. Have a lovely trip, Mum,' she said, pecking Granny on the cheek.

Granny Harumpadunk wiped my mum's kiss off her cheek and smiled down at me. 'Tell you what,' she said. 'I'll see what I can do.'

Half an hour later

I was just sitting down on the sofa for my evening episode of **Future Ratboy** when a car did a fart outside the living room window.

'They're back!' I cried, leaping off the sofa and flying to the front door.

'I cannot believe you've conned your poor old gran into buying you a cuddly sausage dog,' barked my mum, who was trudging up the stairs, carrying a clean pile of my yellow hoodies.

one for each day

Through the blurry glass in the front door I could just see the outline of something amazekeel.

I Future-Ratboy-zoomed my eyes in on whatever my blurry granny was carrying in her hand. It was about the same size as a cuddly sausage dog and had two thin, flappy things sticking out of its head like ears. At the bum end was a long, thin waggly worm that looked exackerly like a tail.

'It's a blooming cuddly sausage dog!' I hollered, turning the handle and opening the door.

Three milliseconds later

'No swearing, Barry!' cried my mum from upstairs as the door opened and I blew off and gasped at the same time, which is never a good idea.

Not that it mattered right now in the history of the whole entire universe amen, because standing in front of me was Granny Harumpadunk, Mr Hodgepodge and a

REAL-LIFE BLOOMING SAUSAGE DOG!

I dropped to my knees as my mum came running down the stairs, her humungous hairdo swaying like a cuddly skyscraper in an earthquake.

'What in the name of . . .' she gasped, blowing off at the same time.

'Unbelievakeelness!' I cried, stumbling to my feet and staggering forward.

I reached my shaking arms out and
Granny Harumpadunk lowered the
sausage dog into my hands. He was
white with black spots and had long
floppy ears the size of pockets.

I snuggled the pooch up against
my jumper. 'A-am I dreaming?'
I stuttered, as my brand new best
friend licked my nose, his little tail
wagging so much it looked like there
were twelve of them.

'Erm, what exactly is happening here?' said my mum.

I plopped the dog on the ground and he started running round my legs, blowing off with excitement like a smelly Catherine wheel.

Granny Harumpadunk chuckled to herself. 'It was the funniest thing, Maureen,' she said. 'Hodge'd parked up outside Roy's Toys and I was just getting out of the car - well I say I was getting out if it, the blinking side door was stuck again, so I was climbing into the back seat - that's the only way out once the old banger's decided to play up . . .'

banger   old banger

'Skip to the bit when you buy my son an ACTUAL REAL-LIFE DOG,' said my mum, her eyelid twitching.

'Well, there I was halfway over the front seat with me bloomers showing when I heard a tap on the passenger side window,' sniggled Granny. 'I said to Hodge, I said, who's that tapping on the window?'

'Who. Was. It,' said my mum, her foot tapping like Nancy's at the disco.

'You'll never guess,' said Granny Harumpadunk. 'My old pal Gladys Foo!'

Gladys Foo

'Gladys Foo?' said my mum, and
I remembered the name from that
sausage dog poster stuck to the
lamp post the week before.

SAUSAGE
DOG FOR
SALE!
Call Gladys Foo
on 555 1485
for more info.

Desmond waddled into the hallway
and the dog zig-zagged over to him
at eight trillion miles an hour, his
whole body wagging.

My mum peered down at him,
snuffling up to Des's fat little belly,
and for a millisecond I spotted a
twinkle in her eye.

baked bean
splodges

'Anyway,' said my gran. 'To cut a long story short, I told Gladys how I was about to buy my little Loser a toy sausage dog and she said, "Why not get a real one?" and I said, "A real one?" and she said, "Yes a real one," and I said, "Where am I gonna get a real one from?" and she said, "Me!"'

'He's perfect!' I said.

'He's going back,' said my mum.

I looked up at my mum, and she went all blurry.

It usually takes me about nine hours to squeeze a single fake tear out of my eye sockets, but this time two ginormous ones immedi-zig-zagged down my nose, like Bunky and Nancy running off to see Anton and Fay.

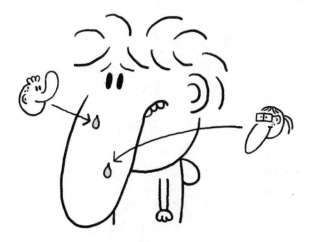

'Oh please Mummy,' I warbled, not even badgering her. 'I can't lose another best friend.'

My mum's eyelid stopped twitching and she peered down at her little Snookyflumps. 'What's wrong, Barry?' she said, all seriously.

And I started to explain.

Give a dog a name

Sometimes just telling the truth is way better than badgering. Especially if the truth makes your mum's eyes go all watery then she bends down and gives you a cuddle and whispers in your ear, 'Alright, you can keep the dog.'

'Oh my unkeelness, thank you, Mum!' I cried, and my brand new pooch bounded over, leaping up at his owner.

I twizzled round on the spot. 'Thank you, Granny!' I smiled, giving her a cuddle too.

totes jelz

'Ahem,' coughed Mr Hodgepodge.

'Er, thanks Mr Hodgepodge,' I said, even though I couldn't see what he'd had to do with the whole thing, apart from driving his half-broken old car down to Roy's Toys at three millimetres per hour.

My mum tapped me on the head. 'You know the deal though, don't you,' she said, and I nodded.

'Don't worry, Mum,' I said, stroking my dog's fuzzy head. 'I'll pick up all his poos and take him for all his walks and feed him and bath him – it'll be like he isn't even here!'

'I must be going blooming barmy,' said my mum, chuckling to herself, and my brand new doggy snuzzled his nose into her ankle.

'No swearing, Mumsicles!' I laughed, scooping him up and giving him a kiss on his shiny wet nose.

'What you gonna call the little fella, Loser?' asked Mr Hodgepodge, and I thought about how he was a sausage dog, and that sausages are one of my favourite things to eat, plus the fact we'd just had sausages for tea.

'Hamburger!' I grinned.

Enter Mr Loser

Just as Granny Harumpadunk and Mr Hodgepodge were about to leave, my dad trudged up to the front door.

'Hello, Ermentrude, hello, Humphrey,' he said, walking through the front door and slipping his boring old work shoes off.

'Ooh don't mind us Kenneth,' said Granny, heading off. 'Enjoy the sausage dog!'

My dad's eyebrows twizzled into two curly squiggles, and what with the little dot-eyes underneath each one, he sort of looked like he had a couple of question marks scribbled right there in the middle of his stubbly face.

'Sausage dog?' he said, watching Granny Harumpadunk's fat bum wobble off down the garden path. 'What's your mother going on about this time, Maureen?'

He twizzled round and glanced at me and Hamburger, grinning up at him, both of us with our tongues hanging out. 'Blooming Nora!' he cried, letting go of his briefcase.

'Language, Kenneth!' said my mum.

'A real life sausage dog!' he said, dropping to his knees. 'It's just what I've always wanted.' I passed Hamburger to my dad, and he cuddled him up to his smelly old suit. 'Ooh, ooh, can we call him Frankie Teacup, Maureen, please can we, pleeease?'

'His name is Hamburger,' I said, as his whole body started waggling, wee spraying out from him in all directions - a bit like that time my dad hammered a nail into the pipe behind the bathroom wall.

'Argh, my suit!' wailed my dad, plonking Hamburger down on the carpet.

'My carpet!' screeched my mum, even though the carpet's orange, and dog wee is yellow, so it doesn't really show.

'Don't worry, Mumsy!' I cried, grabbing the tea towel that was hanging over her shoulder and starting to scrub the carpet with it.

'Not with my Frankie Teacup tea towel!' wailed my dad, yanking it out of my hand.

remember this?

Frankie Teacup

& the saucers

Hamburger charged at the flailing dish cloth like a miniature bull. 'My best vase!' screamed my mum, as he barged into the little wooden table where we drop our keys.

The purple pot toppled over, pouring mouldy old flower water into my dad's briefcase.

'My briefcase!' screeched my dad.

'Relax Kenneth,' I said, trying to calm him down. 'It's not like he's pooed in your shoe, is it?'

And that's when Hamburger squatted his bum over the hole bit of my dad's left shoe and did a poo right in it.

Our little secret

After I'd cleaned out my dad's shoe using my mum's sausage tongs and a whole twin pack of kitchen roll, it was bedtime.

But my mum wouldn't let Hamburger sleep in my room.

'Is my little poochypoos OK?' I shouted for the eight trillionth time, three minutes after she'd tucked me in.

'He. Is. FINE,' shouted my mum from the lounge where she and my dad were giving him a secret snuggle on the sofa. 'Now go to sleep, Barry.'

I lay in bed, listening to the three of them watch Detective Manksniff on the TV below, until the end credits came on and I heard the sound of my mum and dad clearing up their bits and bobs and plumping the sofa cushions up.

'Night night, Frankie Teacup,' said my dad, closing the living room door, and I shook my fist.

'His. Name. Is. Hamburger!' I whisper-shouted in the dark.

I had to wait another eleven minutes for my loserish parents to brush their teeth and do their bedtime wees, and then it all went quiet.

I counted to seventy-nine million then whipped my duvet off, crept down my bed ladder and tip-toed to the door. It creaked as I opened it and I heard a whimper from downstairs.

'Don't worry little doggy, Papa's on his way,' I thought inside my head, wondering if my brand new sausage dog could hear what I was thinking.

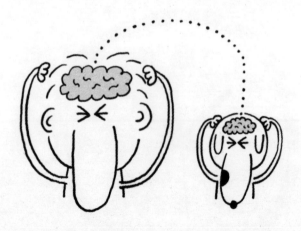

There are thirteen steps on our house's staircase, and I spent about a minute on each one, that's how careful I was making my way down the stairs.

doggy
this
way

'Ruff!' barked Hamburger, leaping off the couch, but only quietly, as if he knew what I was up to was our little secret.

His green eyes glowed like LEDs in the darkness, and I could hear his tail hitting the coffee table as it wagged.

I slumped on to the sofa and he jumped into my lap, nuzzling his head inside my armpit, which luckeely for him isn't all hairy and stinking like my dad's.

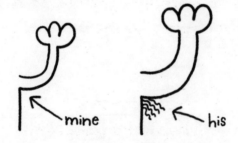

mine

his

I grabbed a cushion and sort of draped it over us, even though cushions are really hard to drape. 'Night night, Hamburger,' I yawned, happy for the first time since I'd become a gooseBarry.

Tutting Snoggles

The next morning I woke up before any of the other Losers and crept upstairs to bed, then got out of it again, pretending I'd been in there all night.

'Fetch the remote control, Hamburger!' I ordered my brand new sausage dog as I strolled into the front room, but he just smiled up at me, his tongue hanging out.

'Very well, doggy,' I said, slumping on the sofa. 'Just stand where my feet are and be my foot stool instead.'

Hamburger jumped on to the sofa, pointed his bum in my face and did a fart.

It looked like teaching him tricks wasn't going to be as easy as I'd thought.

I grabbed the phone and dialled
Bunky's number. 'Bunky, I've got
some amazekeel news!' I said when
he answered.

'Oh yeah?' he said. 'You got yourself
a girlfriend at last?'

Snoggles

I rolled my eyes at Hamburger.
'Don't be a loser,' I said. 'It's a
millikeels times keeler than
a boring old girlfriend.'

'Erm Barry, you're on speakerphone?' said Bunky, and I heard someone in the background, doing a tut.

'Oh,' I said. 'Who's that tutting in the background?'

'It's Fay,' said Bunky.

told you

'Fay?' I yelped. 'As in Fay Snoggles?'

I knew she was his girlfriend at school, but at the weekends too? This was getting ridikeelous.

'So what's this amazekeel news?' asked Bunky, and I smiled down at my hairy new best friend.

'Let's just say I'm not going to be such a gooseBarry anymore,' I said, and I heard Bunky scratch his head.

my phone

his phone

'What in the name of unkeelness are you talking about?' he asked.

'Meet me at the Adventure Playground in twenty minutes and you'll see,' I said. 'And tell Nancy too.'

The Adventure Playground

It was nineteen minutes later and I was walking up to the Adventure Playground in Mogden Park.

'Typikeels,' I grumbled under my breath, spotting Fay Snoggles and Anton Mildew swooping on the rope swings with my ex-best friends, Bunky and Nancy.

'Barry babes!' shouted Sharonella, clip-clopping over. Behind her, Darren was hanging off a rope by his ankles, his head going the same colour as a Cherry Fronkle.

'I'm head over heels for ya, Shaz!' he cried.

Shazza stopped clip-clopping and gasped. 'Oh my days, Baz, is he yours?' she said, pointing at my brand new doggy.

'Shazza, meet Hamburger,' I smiled, and she stuck her hand through the fence and shook his paw like she was one of those gooseberry bushes from the other day.

like a collar

Hamburger sniffed Sharonella's fingers, his four little legs prancing about on the spot all excitedly as Nancy and Anton wandered over.

'A sausage dog?' gasped Nancy.
'Oh Barry, he's just lovely!'

Anton put his hand up like he was at
school. 'Slight problemo,' he sneezed.
'I'm allergic to sausage dogs.'

'That is SO you, Mr Mildew!'
chuckled Nancy.

Darren waddled up, pulling an aerosol can out of his pocket. It had 'Feeko's Jinx for Men' written on the side of it, which is that stuff people with hairy armpits like my dad's spray on themselves so they don't stink so much.

£2.39 from Feeko's

'Let's have a go on that when you're finished, Daz,' said Bunky, and I twizzled round, getting ready to introduce my new best friend to my old one.

Nigel & Snoggy

'Oh my unkeelness!' cried Bunky,
spotting Hamburger.

He grabbed Darren's can of Jinx and
lifted his T-shirt, spraying it on to his
comperleeterly non-hairy armpits.
'So this is the amazkeel news,
eh Barry?'

I nodded, and Fay smiled at my brand
new pooch, but not like she seemed
all that bothered.

'I see what you mean, Baz,' said Bunky, patting Hamburger. 'He really is a millikeels times better than a girlfriend!'

looks like dog

is dog

Fay shoved Bunky. 'Nigel Zuckerberg!' she cried. 'Take that back this instant.'

Bunky nudged Fay with his shoulder. 'Sozzles, Snoggy,' he said, and I almost puked all over my trainers.

I looked at Fay. 'Do you wanna pat him, Snoggles?' I said, pretending to be nice to her. She was my ex-best friend's girlfriend, after all.

Fay shook her head. 'Nah, it's alright,' she said. 'I'm not that into dogs.'

Bunky chucked the Jinx back to Darren. 'Fay collects teaspoons,' he said, like that was something to be proud of.

I tried to peer into Bunky's hairdo and see what was going on inside.

Maybe Fay had swapped his hamster-sized brain for some kind of cuddly heart one instead.

Sharonella fluttered her eyelashes at me and pointed at Darren's aerosol can. 'You should have a spray, Baz,' she said. 'Us girls can't resist the stinx of Jinx!'

Hamburger woofed like he thought it was a good idea.

'No Jinx for Loser,' barked Darren. 'Gotta have a girlfriend to use this stuff.'

'But I've got a sausage dog now,' I said, and Darren snarfled.

'A sausage dog ain't no girlfriend, Barold,' he said, stuffing the can back into his pocket and staring down at Hamburger. 'That fing do any tricks?'

'We're working on a couple,' I said.
'These things take time.'

'Show us then, Barry,' said Nancy.

'Erm . . .' I said, trying to think of
an easy one. 'Sit!' I shouted, because
everyone can make a dog sit.

Hamburger wandered over to Anton
and sniffed his trainer. 'Waaahhh!'
he shrieked. 'Get him away from
me, Mrs V!'

'Leave Anton alone, doggy!' I ordered.

'SOZZAGIS!' yelped Hamburger, his bark sounding a teeny weeny bit like he was saying the word 'sausages'.

'Did he just say sausages?' gasped Sharonella. 'Oh my days Baz, that is SO random!'

I shrugged, pretending like it was no big deal. 'Yeah, that came built-in,' I said, even though it was the first time I'd heard it too.

Fay did a yawn. 'Amazekeels,' she said. 'Can we do something else now?'

'How about Gooseberry Bush Cafe?' said Sharonella, pointing to the other side of Mogden Park. 'Me and my gran go there all the time.'

I Future-Ratboy-zoomed my eyes in on a tiny cottage-shaped building. It was surrounded by loads of little bushes, which going on the name of the place, I guessed were gooseberry ones.

'Oh well that is just perfect,' I mumbled to myself.

Gooseberry Bush Cafe

'Ooh hello, dearies!' warbled an old granny in a black and white waitress outfit as we opened the ancient wooden door and walked into Gooseberry Bush Cafe.

A million wrinkly heads twizzled
round like when you tap on a tank
full of terrapins in a pet shop.

'I'm afraid you won't be able to bring
your little friend in here, love,' said
the waitress, doing a wonky grin
down at Hamburger. 'But there's
plenty of room outside.'

'Come on then gang,' I said, swivelling on the spot, and my trainers squeaked against the shiny concrete floor.

full
nose
swivel

SQUEAK

Hamburger barked, thinking my squeaky shoes were two little yapping dogs or something, which was kind of sweet of him I suppose, but also pretty stupid.

'No offence Barry,' said Anton, which always means someone's about to say something annoying, 'but it's a bit chilly out there for me, and I forgot to bring a sweater.'

Nancy rolled her eyes. 'I told you to pack one, Mr Mildew,' she sighed, sounding like my mum. 'I don't know, you'd forget your head if it wasn't screwed on!'

Fay did a shudder and clung on to Bunky's arm. 'It is a bit chilly. Let's sit inside, shall we Nige?' she said, and Bunky nodded like he was her own personal robot.

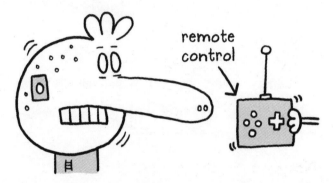

remote control

'FINE,' I said. 'I'll chat to the blooming gooseberry bushes.'

nothing to say →

'Poor old Baz,' said Sharonella. 'Want me to keep you company?'

153

'Loser'll be alright,' said Darren, scraping a chair out. 'Your throne awaits, Madame Sharalumbus,' he grinned.

I went outside and sat down at a table by the window. Through it I could see the six of them inside, chatting away about how much they were all boyfriends and girlfriends with each other.

'Who needs them anyway,' I mumbled down to Hamburger, who was curled up in my lap like a big hairy donut.

'SOZZAGIS!' he barked, and I chuckled all gooseBarryishly.

'Did he just say sausages?' warbled a grumpy voice, and I looked over at the next table. Sitting at it was an old lady wearing angry glasses. 'I hate sausages,' she said.

'O-kaaay,' I said, turning back round to look through the window at my ex-best friends.

'So what's his name?' said the grumpy lady, and I twizzled my head back round to face hers.

'Hamburger,' I said.

'Hamburger?' she barked. 'That's a stupid name for a dog. What kind is he anyway?'

'A sausage dog,' I said.

'Can't stand sausage dogs,' said the old lady, and I smiled at her, hoping that was the end of that.

Not the end of that

The grumpy old lady lifted her bum off her chair all shakily and wobbled over to where I was sitting.

'Mind if I plonk meself down next to you two?' she warbled.

'Er, no?' I said, even though I did.

'Wish I had someone to cuddle like that,' she said, peering down at Hamburger, and I wondered if she really did hate sausage dogs after all.

The wonky-grinned waitress brought out a can of Gooseberry Fronkle for me, a pot of tea for the grumpy old lady and a bowl of water for Hamburger.

'Name's Margot,' said the old lady, slurping her tea. 'Margot Cranky.'

'I'm Barry,' I said, deciding not to say the 'Loser' bit, because everyone always laughs when I do. 'Barry Harumpadunk.'

Barry
Harumpadunk

'Well this is nice I spose,' she grumbled, even though it wasn't nice at all, it was weird. I was sitting outside a granny cafe chatting to a grumpy old lady I didn't even know.

Hamburger jumped off my lap, did a lap around the table, then started lapping at his water. Sorry for saying 'lap' so much in that last sentence, by the way.

'What's your dog's name again?' asked the old lady, even though I'd only just told her three seconds earlier.

'Hamburger,' I said, cracking open my Gooseberry Fronkle. I took a sip and went 'ahhh', the way Margot was doing with her tea.

'Nice sit down and a cup of tea,' she said, pretty much just saying what she was doing out loud.

'Yep,' I said, feeling like I was her husband and we'd comperleeterly run of things to say to each other because of how long we'd been stuck together.

Hamburger stopped lapping and started trotting round and round in a circle like he'd turned into the last bit of water in a bath and was getting ready to swoosh down the plug hole.

'Uh oh,' said Margot. 'You know what that means.'

'What?' I said, because I didn't.

And Margot Cranky smiled for the first time since I'd met her. 'He needs a poo!' she grinned.

See through poo bag

I won't go into detail about what happened next, but let's just say I walked Hamburger over to a tree where he did a ginormous dog poo that really really stank.

as seen on cover

Then I suddenly remembered I didn't have any of those little black plastic bags dog owners carry around to scoop their dogs' poos into.

these

'Oh my goodness gracious me, we are in a pickle aren't we, Burger,' I said, wondering if I was turning into a granny myself.

I ran back to Gooseberry Bush Cafe and stuck my head through the door.

'This is an emergency!' I cried. 'Does anyone have a poo bag?'

The wonky-grinned waitress passed me a couple of see-through plastic bags, which meant I'd be able to see Hamburger's poo through it once I'd done the scooping.

Which was just my blooming luck.

'Thanks,' I said, rushing back outside with my six ex-friends following behind me, but only because they'd finished their Fronkles.

'Nice to meet you, Barry,' warbled Margot Cranky as I zoomed past her, and Darren chuckled.

'So you HAVE got a girlfriend,' he said, pulling the can of Jinx out of his back pocket. 'Wanna spray, Loser?'

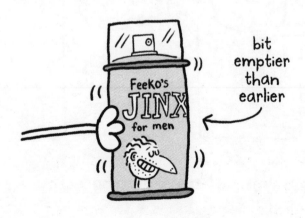

bit
emptier
than
earlier

Feeko's
JINX
for men

I ignored Darren and marched over to the tree where Hamburger had done his poo, putting my hand into one of the see-through bags like it was a glove.

I could feel the warm, squidgy dog poo in my palm as I scooped it up. And the weird thing was, I actukeely quite liked it.

'Now all I need is a poo bin,' I said, spotting one over by the gates. So we all started walking towards it.

Mr Gooseberry

Darren peered at Hamburger's poo, swinging from my hand in its see-through bag. 'You taking that home for din-dins, Loser?' he chuckled.

'Eww, gross!' cried Fay. 'Tell him to stop it, Nigel.'

'Cut it out, Dazza,' said Bunky, and Anton patted him on the back.

'I've got to say, Nigel - Fay's really helped you grow as a person over the last couple of weeks,' he said. 'Me and Mrs V were only talking about it last night.'

Hamburger looked over at Anton like he thought he was a comperleet loseroid, which he is. 'SOZZAGIS!' he barked, and I opened my mouth to try and join in with the chat.

'Yeah, it's the same with Hamburger,'
I said. 'He's really helped me learn
how to, erm . . . pick up poos.'

Nancy peered at me through her
glasses. 'I don't think you can
compare a sausage dog to a real-life
girlfriend or boyfriend, Barry,'
she said.

oh yeah?

boyfriend   girlfriend

Darren nodded as we walked up to
the poo bin. 'Yeah, Loser, are you
saying I should be picking up Shazza's
poos or something?' he snuffled, and
Shazza punched his arm.

'Don't listen to him, Baz,' she said.
But Nancy was right. Having a
sausage dog didn't stop me being a
gooseBarry. If anything, it'd made
me into even more of one.

'I think it's time I got Hamburger back
for dinner,' I mumbled, chucking the
poo bag at the bin.

And of keelse, it comperleeterly
missed.

Evening poo

'How was Frankie Teacup today?'
said my dad when I got home.

'His. Name. Is. Blooming. HAMBURGER!'
I cried, slumping into the sofa.

'Language, Barry!' shouted my mum.

'And don't forget to feed that dog,
young man.'

I trudged into the kitchen and splodged half a can of Feeko's Dog Hamburgers into Hamburger's bowl.

Then I took him out for his evening walk, where he did three wees - one against a boring old lamp post, one against a tree and one straight down a drain.

We were just strolling back to our house when he started to twirl round in a circle on the pavement, and we all know what that means.

I pulled see-through plastic bag number two out of my pocket and slipped it over my hand. 'Blooming sausage dog,' I mumbled to myself, reaching down and grabbing the poo.

Which is when I realised the bag had a hole in it.

Barry Loser's lonely Sunday

Seeing as that day had been a Saturday, the next one was a Sunday.

Hamburger had kept me up half the night with his barking, and because of that I was in a bit of a bad mood.

Even though it was going to make me feel like a comperleet and utter gooseBarry, I decided to find out what my ex-best friends were up to and tag along.

I dialled Nancy's number and her mum answered.

'Hi Mrs V, is Nancy there?' I said in my talking-to-someone-else's-mum-on-the-phone voice.

'Ooh hello, Barry,' she said. 'Nancy just popped out with Anton. I think they were meeting up with Bunky and Fay.'

'Okay, not a problem at all!' I smiled, hanging up.

My nose drooped and my eyebrows tilted into their angry positions.

'Well that's just fan-blooming-tastic, isn't it,' I grumbled.

Hamburger woofed and tilted
his head, smiling up at his master.

'What're you so happy about?'
I growled, grabbing his lead. 'Spose
I'd better take you out to do your
morning poo.'

We strolled down to Mogden Park,
my eyeballs dotting around in all
directions, secretly looking out for
Bunky and Nancy and their stupid old
girlfriend and boyfriend.

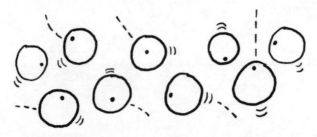

But I couldn't see them anywhere.

I spotted a stick lying on the floor and remembered back to before I had a sausage dog, when I'd been planning to teach it tricks.

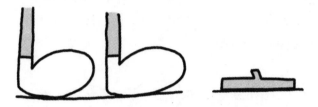

I picked the stick up and threw it. 'Fetch, doggy!' I cried, even though fetching a stick isn't even really a trick.

Hamburger jumped off the ground and twizzled his legs in mid-air, the way people do in cartoons when they're about to zoom off.

Then he zoomed off - in the comperleet wrong direction.

'Blooming brillikeels,' I said. 'Can't even fetch a flipping stick.'

After that we headed over to the
Adventure Playground.

'Barold!' cried a smug, ugly voice, and
I peered up at Gordon Smugly, about
to jump on to the rope which Stuart
Shmendrix was already swinging on.

'WAAAHHH!!!' screamed Stuart as
Gordon landed on top of him.

Gordon jumped off the rope and
strolled over, Stuart wobbling
after him.

'Now there's a pathetic looking beast if I ever did see one,' drawled Smugly, pointing his nose at Hamburger, and I snarled at him, because nobody messes with a member of the Loser family and gets away with it.

'Where's Bunky and Nancy?' asked Stuart, giving Hamburger a pat on the head.

'I don't think I'm in their gang anymore,' I muttered, mostly to myself.

Gordon stroked his chin and looked me up and down, as if I was a gooseberry he was thinking about chomping.

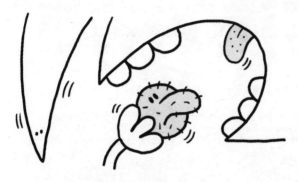

'Me and Shmendrix are off to the cinema after this,' he said. 'Spose we'd let you come along if you behaved yourself.'

And even though I don't really like Gordon and Stuart that much, and sausage dogs aren't allowed in Mogden Cinema, I immedikeely said yes.

Mogden Cinema

The keel thing about living in Mogden is that everything is twenty minutes away from everything else.

The unkeel thing about Mogden Cinema as we walked up to it nineteen minutes and thirty eight seconds later was that my ex-best friends and their stupid girlfriend and boyfriend were **STANDING OUTSIDE IT** with the blooming Shazzonofskis.

My legs started to wobble as
I staggered up to them all, chatting
to each other like a six-pack of
Evil Fronkles.

'What in the name of an entire
punnet of mouldy gooseberries are
YOU LOT doing here WITHOUT ME?'
I boomed.

I knew they'd gone out somewhere
together, but not the blooming
cinema!

'Barry!' said Bunky, looking all guilty. 'What're you doing here?'

Gordon chuckled to himself. 'Well this is awkward,' he smiled.

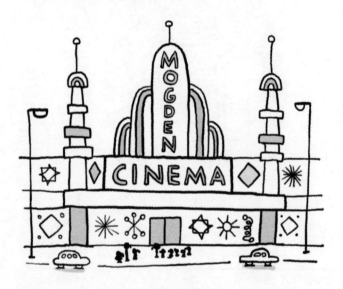

Anton, who hadn't forgotten his sweater this time, did a little cough. 'Let me explain,' he said.

But I wasn't in the mood. 'Save your breath, "Mr Mildew",' I snarled. 'I've had enough of you all!'

I stared up at the poster for the film we were about to watch and shook my head.

'Oh well that makes sense doesn't it,' I said, reading what it was called.

Disaster Strikes!

Darren pushed the big glass door of the cinema open. 'Disaster Strikes! starts in five minutes,' he said. 'You losers can carry on your little squabble afterwards.'

I stared at Darren and noticed he was carrying a six-pack of Cherry Fronkle, which was probably how many cans he needed to get through a film.

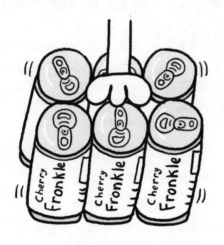

'Come on Barold,' said Gordon. 'Forget about that lot - me and Stuart are your best friends now.'

'Good point, Gordon,' I said, tucking Hamburger into my hoodie and zipping it up so only his nose was sticking out.

x-ray

'No woofing for the next three hours please,' I whispered to my pooch. Then I turned the volume up on my voice so Bunky and Nancy could hear. 'Papa's watching a movie with his NEW BEST FRIENDS.'

Bunky rolled his eyes. 'Oh come on Barry,' he said. 'Don't be like that.'

I opened my mouth to say something, but Darren's voice came out.

'Extra large sweet popcorn,' he said to the spotty teenager behind the counter. 'Just like my scrummy girlfriend!'

'You calling me extra large?' snapped Sharonella, and everyone in the queue turned round to start enjoying their argument.

The cinema manager, who was a fat man wearing green-tinted glasses, strutted over and frowned down at Darren. 'What exactly do you think you're doing?' he asked.

'I am having an argument wiv my girlfriend,' said Darren.

'I'm talking about those,' said the manager, staring at the six-pack of Cherry Fronkles. 'You can't bring cans into the Multiplex.'

He pointed at a ginormous Fronkle machine where you could pour yourself a cup for nine million times the price of a can.

Inside my hoodie Hamburger wriggled. 'Shush puppy,' I whispered, even though he wasn't exackerly making any noise, it was just that the hoodie was jiggling around a bit.

Now I don't know if you know this, but when somebody's hoodie jiggles around a bit, it kind of catches peoples' eyes.

The ones inside the manager's green-tinted glasses swivelled over to look at me, and I imagined I must've looked even more like a gooseBarry than normal, what with the colour of his lenses.

'Your hoodie is moving,' he said, like he couldn't believe the words coming out of his mouth.

And that's when Hamburger barked **'SOZZAGIS!'** and stuck his head out of my jumper.

Actual real life disaster strikes

It was twenty minutes, I mean seconds, later and we were all standing outside Mogden Cinema. All of us apart from Gordon and Stuart that is, seeing as they'd snuck off before the Manager spotted Hamburger.

Inside my hoodie, Hamburger was
barking and scrabbling around.
'Oh be quiet, you stupid little mutt!'
I growled, pulling him out and
plonking him on the pavement.

'Nice one, Loser!' burped Darren,
cracking open one of his
cans. 'Now we
can't watch
Disaster Strikes!
All because
of your
stupid little
doggy-woggy.'

'What are you talking about, Darrenofski?' I cried. 'If it wasn't for your six-pack that bloke never would've spotted Hamburger!'

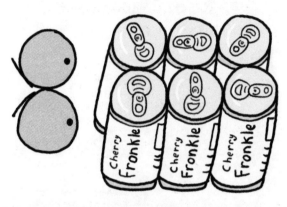

Anton, who looked like a comperleet grandad in his big woolly sweater, opened his mouth. 'Actually it was Sharonella who originally caught the Manager's attention,' he said.

'Oh right, so you're saying it's my fault are you, "Mr Mildew"?' squawked Sharonella. 'Dazzy, you gonna let him talk to me like that?'

Darren put his arm round his girlfriend.

'Shhhh, my Smoochypoos,' he cooed. 'Ooh, how I hate to see you this way.'

I turned round to puke all over Bunky and Nancy's trainers.

'By the way,' I said to my ex-best friends. 'I'm still waiting to hear why you lot were going to the cinema without me and Hamburger.'

I pointed down at my little doggy, sitting on the pavement, and everybody gasped.

Which was weird at first. Until I looked down and realised he'd run away.

Lost dog

'Hamburger!' I screamed. 'My little poochy's disappeared!'

'Maybe he heard you calling him a stupid mutt?' burped Darren.

'Actually I think he said stupid LITTLE mutt,' said Anton.

Bunky held his hands up in the air. 'Guys, you're not helping the situation,' he said. 'We've got to find Barry's sausage dog!'

'Why should we help him?' growled Darren. 'I thought he'd had enough of us all.'

I was dancing around on the spot like I needed a wee, not that I did. I just wanted to get on with finding Hamburger. 'I was just annoyed, that's all,' I warbled. 'Because you'd all met up without me and everything!'

Nancy put her arm round my shoulders, doing her face she does when she's feeling sorry for me.

'We would've invited you, Barry,' she said. 'But everyone knows dogs aren't allowed in Mogden Cinema.'

'It's not just that,' I said. 'You've been making me feel like a gooseBarry all week.'

They all did their confused faces.

'I thought getting a dog'd make me part of the gang again,' I carried on. 'But even that didn't work.'

Bunky sighed. 'Sorry, Barry,' he said. 'We didn't know you felt like that.'

'You didn't?' I asked, and they nodded, all apart from Darren.

'Course not, Baz,' said Sharonella, fluttering her eyelashes at me. 'We love you, ya little Loser!'

'Right, enough of this slushy stuff,' said Nancy, grabbing Anton and me. 'We'll go this way.' She pointed up Mogden High Street towards Bruce the butcher's. 'You lot look down there.'

Bunky & Fay and Shazza & Dazza twizzled round on the spot and zoomed off.

'We'll call you if we find him,' cried Sharonella over her shoulder.

But to cut a long story short, they didn't.

'Any luck?' I asked half an hour later, panting from running around Mogden like an old granny with her knickers on fire.

Darren shook his head. 'Nope,' he burped.

Anton scratched his bum. 'Looks like it's time for plan B,' he said, and I turned to face him.

'What's that?' I said, my ears
pricking up like a sausage dog's.

'Lost Dog posters!' smiled Anton.

'Lost Dog posters?' I cried. 'Anyone
could've come up with that!'

Nancy pushed her glasses up her nose. 'Mr Mildew's just trying to help, Barry,' she said.

'You're right,' I sighed, feeling like a bit of a cranberry, or whatever fruit it is people call people who aren't being very grateful.

me

Feeko's
Ungrateful
cranberries
may contain
slop

'Come on, let's do this,' I said, heading back to my house to make some Lost Dog posters.

Lost Dog posters

It was weird, sticking Lost Dog posters on lamp posts all over Mogden.

It felt like only days ago I'd spotted the one saying 'Sausage dog for sale'.

Everywhere I looked, things reminded me of Hamburger.

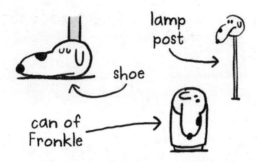

lamp post

shoe

can of Fronkle

Like when I was sticking a Lost Dog poster to the boring old lamp post outside Bruce the butcher's and I spotted a stack of plastic hamburgers piled up in his window.

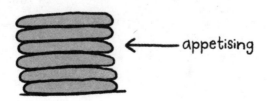

appetising

Or when I was sticking another Lost Dog poster to another lamp post three billiseconds later while a dog was doing a real-life wee up against it and all over my trainers a bit too.

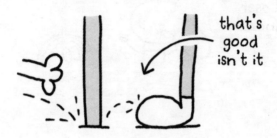

that's good isn't it

'I'm sorry, Hamburger,' I whispered inside my head, and I hoped wherever he was, he could hear what I was thinking.

just reusing drawing

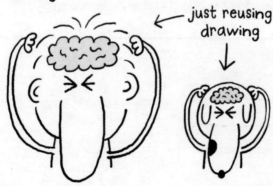

'That's us all out of posters,' said
Bunky, him and Fay walking up to
me twelve trillion hours later.

the old
Loser
shnozzle

Snoggles put her arm round my
shoulders, even though I hadn't said
she could. 'Don't worry Barry, we'll
find him,' she said, and I gave her
a fake smile, thinking maybe she
wasn't all that bad after all.

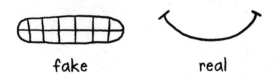

fake   real

Nancy and Anton strolled over.
'I calculate we've flyered ninety-
seven percent of lamp posts in the
Greater Mogden Borough,' said
Mr Mildew.

'Thanks, gang,' I said, even though
they weren't all there. 'Anyone know
where the Shazzonofskis are?'

Just then I heard a wheezing noise
from behind me.

I swivelled round and spotted
Sharonella running towards me with
Darren behind her, his face as red as
a Diet Cherry Fronkle.

'Bazzy!' she cried. 'I've just seen
my gran - I think I know where
Hamburger is!'

Weirdo question

'WHERE IS HE?' I cried in all capitals.

Sharonella was folded over in half, trying to catch her breath.

'Tell me, Shazza!' I boomed. 'I've got to know where my smoochy little poochy-poos is!'

Darren, who was lying on the pavement, his chest going up and down like a bouncy castle, raised a hand. 'He's . . . in . . . an . . .' he gasped.

what he looked like

'In a what?' I wailed. A cloud bubbled up above my head, a video playing inside it of Hamburger inside a rubbish truck, the jaws closing down on him like a giant robot eating a hot dog.

Sharonella straightened back up, her hair sticking out like an exploding party popper.
'He's in an old people's home,' she said.

what she looked like

'An old people's home?' gasped Bunky. 'But he's a dog, not an old person!'

Darren, who was still lying on his back, opened his mouth. 'Some old lady found a sausage dog wandering around Mogden,' he said. 'She took him back there - and she's not giving him back!'

I sat down on a nearby bench, blowing off into the planks. 'How does your gran know all this?' I warbled.

Sharonella plonked her bum down next to mine. 'She was visiting her friend who lives at the old people's home,' she started to explain. 'I say friend - she's got millions of them there. Practically her whole gang's living in the place these days.'

I rolled my eyes. 'Go on . . .' I said.

'I'd popped home for a wee,' said Sharonella. 'And was telling her about Hamburger, how you'd lost him and everything. And Gran - well, she asks me this weirdo question.'

'What was the weirdo question, Shaz?' asked Nancy, and we all went quiet, waiting for Sharonella to tell us.

'She asked me if he could speak English,' she said.

Mogden Home for Old Grannies and Grandads

Bunky did his confused face. 'But dogs can't speak English,' he said. 'Only people can.'

'Ah ha!' I said. 'But Hamburger can say SOZZAGIS!'

Sharonella clicked her fingers and pointed at me. 'Exactamondo,' she smiled. 'My gran says this old lady's new dog can say SAUSAGES!'

'That's Hamburger!' I cried. 'Where's the old people's home?'

Shaz got off the bench and started jogging. 'About twenty minutes this way!'

'Blooming Nora, not again!' panted Darren as the gang started to follow.

We ran for ten minutes, which is how long you have to run to get somewhere twenty minutes away.

'This is the place,' said Sharonella, and I spotted a sign that read 'Mogden Home for Old Grannies and Grandads'.

'How're we gonna get in there?' burp-gasped Darren, opening can number two of his six-pack. 'We're nowhere near wrinkly enough!'

regular
Darren

raisin
flavour

Sharonella strolled through the gates like she owned the place. 'No problemo,' she smiled. 'I've been here a trillion times with my gran, I'll just tell them we're visiting one of her pals.'

'Ooh hello, Shazza,' smiled the lady behind the counter as we burst through the main entrance.

'Mornkeels, Jackie,' said Sharonella, all casual. 'Just popping in to see Ernie.'

Jackie checked her computer. 'Ernie's out I'm afraid,' she said. 'He's at the cinema watching Disaster Strikes!'

Sharonella blinked. 'Oh,' she said. 'In that case we'll see Vera.'

'Okeydokes,' said Jackie, and we walked up to two glass doors that slid open automatically. 'But just so you know,' she called after us, 'it's the OAP disco in twenty minutes!'

223

The OAP disco

You know how it only took us ten minutes to run to the old people's home?

Well it took about twenty five to find the old lady who'd stolen Hamburger - that's how much of a maze Mogden Home for Old Grannies and Grandads was.

'There he is!' cried Anton as we turned a corner into a little hall.

Music was playing and the lights were turned down. There were chairs all the way round the edge, and at one end of the room somebody had stacked a pyramid of teacups on top of a snack table.

Grannies and grandads were gliding round arm-in-arm on the dance floor, their walking sticks propped up against the walls.

And there in a corner, sitting all on her own, was a familikeels old lady with a grumpy face and a sausage dog in her lap.

doesn't look that sad

'It's Margot Cranky!' I gasped, rewinding my brain to the other day when she'd said she wanted a dog to cuddle. 'She's the one who stole my Hamburger!'

Bunky grabbed me and ran across
the dance floor, the gang following
behind. 'Hide!' he cried, ducking behind
the pyramid of teacups. 'If she spots
us she'll scarper.'

'What we gonna do now then?'
burped Darren, eyeing up a plate of
Feeko's Chocolate Digestives. 'That old
lady ain't budging from her seat.'

I scratched my nose, trying to come up with one of my brilliant and amazing plans, but the thought bubble above my head was empty.

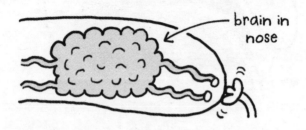

brain in nose

'Bingo!' whispered Anton, and what with his woolly sweater and everything, he looked just like a real-life grandad. 'I think I've had an idea.'

grandad outfit

Darren reached across and grabbed a biscuit, stuffing it in his mouth.

'Go on then, Mr Mildew,' he snuffled, a chocolate goatee zig-zagged round his mouth. 'Tell us what it is.'

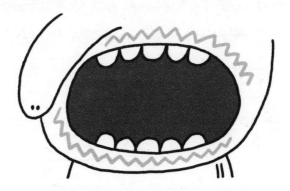

Anton smiled to himself and started to explain.

229

Mr Mildew's terrible idea

'You have got to be kidding me!'
I cried, once Anton had told us
his plan, which was this:

1. I put a disguise on
2. Go up to Margot Cranky
3. Ask her for a dance
4. She leaves Hamburger on the chair
5. Bunky steals him back

Bunky sniggled. 'I think it's pretty keel,'
he said.

'But what about Hamburger?' I said.
'He'll spot me straight away and
start weeing himself with excitement.
Old Cranky'll know something's up,
for sure.'

me →

him
spotting
me

her
spotting
him
spotting
me

Anton grinned. 'She'll just think her
brand new sausage dog likes you,'
he said. 'Which can only be a good
thing.'

'Ugh, I cannot believe this happening to me,' I groaned. 'It's bad enough dancing with girls. But boogying with a granny?'

The song that was playing stopped and a familikeels-sounding fingernail tapped the microphone.

TAP TAP

'This is DJ Dongles coming at ya on the ones and twos,' boomed a voice through the speakers. 'And here's a little something for all you lovers out there!'

'Oh my unkeelness,' cried Nancy.
'It's Mrs Dongle!'

'Ooh-ooh, kids!' she mouthed, spotting us behind the teacups. 'What are you lot doing here?'

nicked off
page 18

'I could ask you the same thing,' I mouthed back, as she pressed a button and Banana Moon started to warble out of the speakers.

Bunky grabbed a biscuit and licked the chocolate bit, then he reached across and drew a moustache along my lip. 'Eww, gross!' I cried, sounding like Fay Snoggles.

Anton grabbed a flat cap some grandad had left on a chair while he'd gone for a boogie and plonked it on my head. 'Just needs one more thing,' he said, pulling off his woolly sweater and passing it to me.

'Have a go on this for good luck, Loser,' smiled Darren as I put Anton's grandad sweater on, and he handed me his can of Jinx.

now even emptier

'Thanks, Daz,' I said, spraying the armpit bits of Anton's jumper.

Then Bunky gave me a shove and I stumbled on to the dance floor.

Chatting up a granny

I zig-zagged across the dance floor, trying not to bump into any granny or grandad bums. Then I popped out the other side, face to face with Hamburger.

'SOZZAGIS!' he barked, his whole body starting to wag.

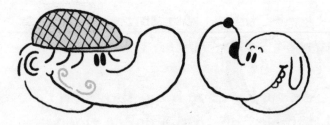

'Ho ho, your dog seems to like me!'
I boomed in my best grandad voice.

I glanced to my right and spotted
Bunky, creeping round to snatch
the little pooch as soon as Margot
plonked him down.

The grumpy old lady stared through
her angry glasses at me. 'Do I know
you?' she said, crunching on a
chocolate digestive.

I peered into her hairdo, trying to work out what was going on inside it. 'I'm here with Ernie,' I smiled.

'Ernie's gone to the pictures,' said Margot, looking all suspicious.

'I mean Vera,' I said, still staring at her hair. It reminded me of something, but I couldn't work out what.

Margot screwed her face up. 'I hate Vera,' she said, stroking Hamburger, who was wriggling in her arms, trying to get back to his owner.

'Why do you hate her?' I asked, not that I really cared. I was just putting off asking her for a dance.

'I hate 'em all,' said Margot, nodding at the dance floor. 'Look at the blooming show-offs, all paired off and lovey-dovey. Makes you sick, dunnit.'

And that's when I realised what her hairdo looked like: a gooseberry bush!

'Well blow me down with a pair of knickers!' I muttered to myself all grandadishly. 'Margot Cranky's a blooming gooseberry just like me!'

'What're you looking so pleased
about?' she asked, as I reached
my hand out, spotting
Bunky twenty
centimetres
away.

'Would you like to dance?' I asked,
and her angry glasses turned
all happy.

Dancing with a granny

The weird thing about boogying with a granny while my best friend stole my sausage dog back is, I actukeely quite enjoyed it.

'What's your name, old man?' she asked as we swung round the dance floor. Hamburger smiled at us from Margot's chair, licking up biscuit crumbs.

'Barry,' I said without thinking, and her eyebrows shot a centimetre up her wrinkly forehead.

'That's funny,' she said. 'I met a Barry yesterday. He was about your height, too.'

'Strange how these things happen, isn't it,' I chuckled, actukeely sounding like a real-life grandad.

Margot leaned back a millimetre and looked me up and down. 'You're very short for a grown-up,' she said. 'What's your second name?'

Behind her, Bunky had reached her chair. He scooped Hamburger into his arms and gave me a thumbs-up.

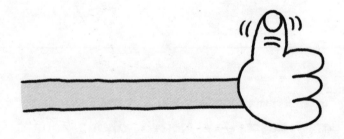

'Loser!' I said, waiting for Margot to realise I was the one whose dog she'd stolen.

But instead of that, she just shook her head. 'Silly me,' she chuckled to herself. 'For a second there I thought I'd found the owner of that dog.'

She pointed over her shoulder to where Hamburger had been sitting. 'His name was Barry Harumpadunk though.'

funny old chair, innit

I rewound my brain to the other day, when I'd pretended my second name was Harumpadunk. 'That's me!' I cried. 'I'm Barry Harumpadunk!'

rememboid?

'Eh?' said Margot. 'I thought you said your name was Loser?'

'It is,' I said. 'I mean, that's my real name. I only pretended it was Harumpadunk so you wouldn't laugh.'

'But Harumpadunk's even worse than Loser,' said Margot, her glasses going all confused.

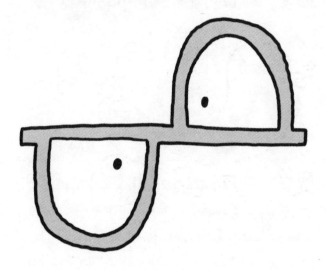

I ripped my flat cap off my head and wriggled out of Anton's jumper.

'Wait a millikeels,' I said, wiping the chocolate moustache off my lip. 'So you didn't steal Hamburger after all?'

The Doggy Walk Wiggle

By the time Margot had explained
how she'd found Hamburger walking
around Mogden the day before, then
phoned round everywhere trying to
find a boy called Barry Harumpadunk
so she could give him back, Banana
Moon had finished playing and the
lights had come back on.

DJ Dongles tapped her mike. 'That's it for this week, ladies and gents,' boomed her voice. 'See you same time next Sunday!'

Bunky passed me Hamburger and I gave him a cuddle, the way my mum gives me one every day after school.

'Oh Burger,' I cooed. 'I'm sorry I got all grumpy with you. Will you ever forgive me?'

Hamburger woofed and licked my face. 'I reckon he still likes you,' chuckled Margot. 'Hamby, fetch Barry a biccie, there's a good pooch.'

The little dog jumped out of my arms and zig-zagged over to the snack table, coming back with a Feeko's chocolate digestive in his mouth. He dropped it at my feet and grinned up at me.

'How in the name of keelness did you teach him to do that?' I gasped, picking up the drool-covered snack.

'Easy,' said Margot, whipping a non-drool-covered biscuit out of her pocket and throwing it into Hamburger's mouth. 'I spoil him!'

Bunky and Nancy wandered over with Fay and Anton, Darren wobbling behind. 'So...' said Nancy. 'Everything alright with us now?'

'Yeah,' I smiled. 'Who cares if I'm a gooseBarry. It doesn't stop us being friends ... does it?'

'Course not!' smiled Bunky, and I was just about to ask where Sharonella was when I spotted her on the other side of the room, whispering something into DJ Dongles's ear.

Mrs Dongle nodded and clicked the lights back off.

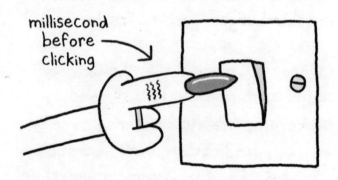

millisecond before clicking

'I'm dying!' croaked an old grandad from the dance floor, then he realised it was just the lights going out.

Sharonella skipped over to us and grinned. 'Ready for the Doggy Walk Wiggle?' she said, and DJ Dongles pressed a button on her music machine.

'Hey, Margot,' I said, as the **Future Ratboy** music started to boom out of the speakers. 'Anytime you wanna see Hamburger, just let me know.'

Margot gave me a thumbs-up and Hamburger wagged his tail, wee spraying everywhere.

I looked at my friends, all jiggling on the dance floor, and smiled. 'I love you guys,' I thought inside my head.

And even though I knew they couldn't hear me, I reckon they definitely knew.

The end

BTW, everyone split up a week later.

About the author and drawer

Jim Smith is the keelest kids' book author and drawer in the whole wide world amen.

He graduated from art school with first class honours (the best you can get) and went on to create the branding for a keel little chain of coffee shops.

He's also designed cards and gifts under the name Waldo Pancake.

Jim's dream job, apart from writing and drawing stupid little stories, would be to design a can of drink.